Black Beauty

ANNA SEWELL

Adapted by ELEANOR GRAHAM VANCE

Illustrated by PHOEBE ERICKSON

Prepared under the supervision of JOSETTE FRANK,
Children's Book Adviser of the Child Study Association of America

---

RANDOM HOUSE · NEW YORK

This title was originally catalogued by the library of Congress as follows: Sewell, Anna, 1820-1878. Black Beauty; adapted by Eleanor Vance; illustrated by Phoebe Erickson. Prepared under the supervision of Josette Frank. New York, Random House, 1949. 62 p. illus. (part col.) 29 cm. I. Vance, Eleanor (Graham) 1908- II. Title. PZ10.3.S38Bl 58
49–11994* ISBN: 0-394-80637-9 ISBN: 0-394-90637-3 (lib. bdg.)

BLACK BEAUTY

THE first place Black Beauty could remember was a big green meadow where there were other young horses like himself—and, of course, his mother, whose name was Duchess. Their master, Farmer Gray, was a good, kind man, who lived near by in a house by the roadside.

Black Beauty loved to run by his mother's side, drink her warm milk, and lie down close to her at night. As soon as he was old enough to eat grass, his mother went out to work in the daytime and left him to play in the meadow. But she always came back to him before dark.

3

The other colts in the meadow were older than Black Beauty.
He used to run with them, and they all had fun playing together,
galloping around the field as hard as they could go. Sometimes,
though, the colts would bite and kick as well as gallop.

One day when the colts had been very rough in their play, Duchess whinnied to Black Beauty to come to her. "I want you to pay attention to what I am going to say," she told him. "The colts who live here are good colts, but they have not learned manners. Your father was a fine horse, and your grandfather won important races; your grandmother had the sweetest temper of any horse I ever knew, and I think you have never seen me kick or bite. I hope you will grow up gentle and good, and never learn bad ways. Do your work with a good will, lift up your feet when you trot, and never bite or kick even in play."

6

Black Beauty hung his head at this gentle scolding, but he never forgot his mother's words. He knew she was a wise old horse, and that the master was very fond of her. The master gave all his horses good food, a comfortable place to live, and spoke kindly to them, but Duchess and Black Beauty were his favorites.

There was a farm boy, Dick, who worked for Farmer Gray and sometimes came into the field to pick blackberries from the hedge. When he had eaten all he wanted, he would have what he called fun with the colts, throwing stones and sticks at them to make them gallop. Sometimes the stones hurt them.

One day he was at this game, and did not know that the master was in the next field, watching him.

Over the hedge the master jumped and, catching Dick by the arm, gave him a good shaking. Black Beauty and the other colts trotted up nearer to see what was going on.

"Bad boy!" the master was saying. "Bad boy to chase the colts! Here, take your money and go home. I do not want you working on my farm."

So the colts never saw Dick any more. Old Daniel, who looked after them, was just as gentle as the master. So the colts were well cared for and contented.

8

Several years passed, and Black Beauty was beginning to grow into a handsome young horse. His coat, which was bright black, had become fine and soft. He had one white foot and a pretty white star on his forehead.

"You are well-named, Black Beauty," the master said to him one day, "for you are as black as you are beautiful. But I shall not sell you until I have broken you in. Boys ought not to work like men, and colts ought not to work like horses until they are quite grown up."

When Black Beauty was four years old a man came to look at him. The man's name was Squire Gordon. He examined Black Beauty all over and then said, "I like him. When he has been well broken in, I shall buy him." The master said he would break Black Beauty in himself, as he would not want him to be frightened or hurt.

So, the very next day Black Beauty began learning what was meant by being "broken in." He had of course been used to being led about the fields and lanes by a halter, but now he was to have a bit and a bridle. The bit, thought Black Beauty, was a nasty thing. It was a great piece of cold hard steel that was pushed into his mouth between his teeth and over his tongue, with the ends coming out at the corners of his mouth and held fast there by straps over his head, under his throat, around his nose, and under his chin. Black Beauty hated it at first, but what with his master's pats, kind words and gentle ways, he soon got used to wearing his bit and bridle. Black Beauty was also taught to carry a person on his back and to go

quietly just the way his rider wanted him to go. He had to learn to wear harness and to stand still while it was being put on, and to pull a cart around behind him. He had to learn not to be frightened by strange things he saw on the road.

As part of his training, Black Beauty was sent away for a couple of weeks to live in a meadow near a railway track. Some sheep and cows were there, and Black Beauty

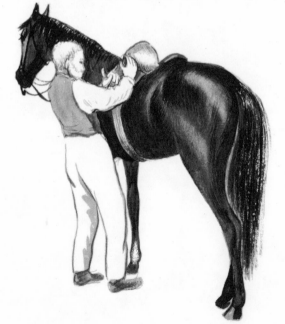

was turned in among them. At first the trains nearly scared the little horse out of his wits. What was this great black monster that came shrieking and puffing out of nowhere? When he heard it, Black Beauty galloped to the opposite side of the field and stood trembling and snorting. But as the other trains went by and he saw that they never came into the field or tried to hurt him, he began to get as used to them as the cows and sheep were. And so, thanks to his wise master's training, Black Beauty never again had any fear of steam engines or trains.

13

The master trained Black Beauty in other ways, too. He often drove him in double harness with his mother, for Duchess was a steady mare and could teach him how to go better than a strange horse might.

Duchess tried to give her son good advice.

"The better you behave, the better you will be treated," she said, "but I'm sorry to tell you that there are many kinds of men. There are good, thoughtful men like our master, and there are others who are cruel and bad, and some who are foolish and careless. I hope you will fall into good hands. But wherever you go, and whatever kind of master you get, always do your best."

And so on a bright and sunny day in May, when Black Beauty had been thoroughly broken in, a man came to take him to his new home at Squire Gordon's in Birtwick Park.

"Good-by, Black Beauty," said the master. "Be a good horse."

Black Beauty could not say "good-by," so he put his nose into the master's hand. The master patted him kindly, and then Black Beauty left his first home.

AT Birtwick Park the stable was big and airy, with four good stalls in it. The first stall was the biggest, and into this fine box the groom led Black Beauty, gave him some oats, patted him kindly, and left him.

After he had eaten the good oats, Black Beauty looked around. In the next stall stood a little fat gray pony.

"How do you do?" said Black Beauty. "What is your name?"

"My name is Merrylegs," said the pony. "Are you going to live next door to me?"

"Yes," said Black Beauty.

"Well, then," Merrylegs said, "I hope you are good-tempered; I don't like anyone next door who bites."

Just then the head of a tall chestnut mare came up from the stall beyond. The ears were laid back, and there was an ill-tempered look in the eyes.

"So you're the one who has turned me out of my stall!" she exclaimed. "A colt like you turning a lady out of her own home!"

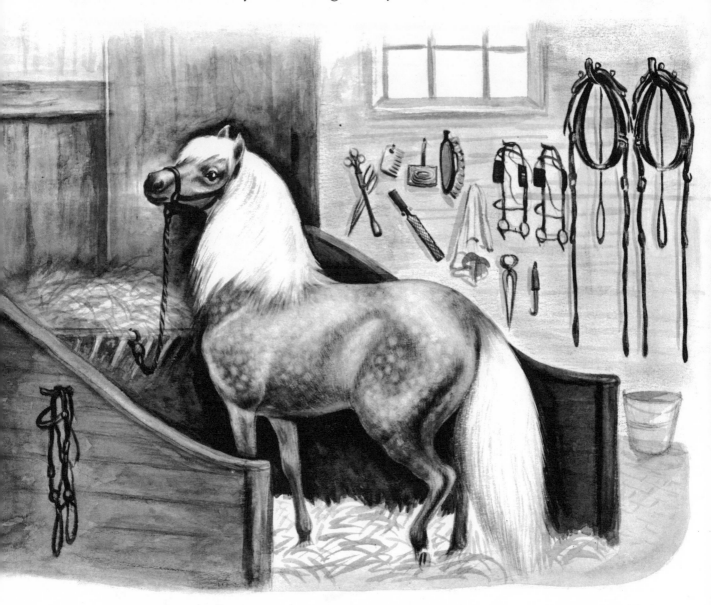

"I beg your pardon," said Black Beauty. "I haven't turned anybody out. The man who brought me put me here. And as to my being a colt, I'm four years old and I'm a grown-up horse. I've never had a quarrel with anybody, and it is my wish to live at peace."

The mare said, "We shall see," and turned her back. Later that day, when she was out of the stable, Merrylegs told Black Beauty all about her.

"The trouble is that Ginger has a bad habit of biting and snapping. When she was in your box she used to snap so much that Miss Flora and Miss Jessie were afraid to come into the stable. They are very fond of me and I hope they will come again now, if you do not bite or snap."

Black Beauty told Merrylegs that he never bit anything but grass, hay and corn.

"It's just a bad habit with Ginger," Merrylegs went on. "She says no one was ever good to her, and why shouldn't she bite? People must have been very unkind to her before she came here. But perhaps she will be good-tempered from now on. You see," he said with a wise look, "I'm twelve years old; and I can tell you there isn't a better place in the country for a horse than this. So it's all Ginger's fault that she didn't stay in that box."

In a very short time Black Beauty felt quite at home among his new friends at Birtwick Park. John, the groom, seemed to know just how a horse feels; and when he cleaned Black Beauty, he knew the tender places and the ticklish places. James, the stable boy, was just as pleasant and gentle in his way.

And of course there was Merrylegs, who was so cheerful, plucky and good-tempered. Miss Jessie and Miss Flora used to ride him about in the orchard and have fine games with him and their little dog Frisky.

20

Not long after his arrival, Black Beauty was taken out with Ginger to pull the carriage. He wondered how they would get on together, but she behaved very well. When they went up a hill, instead of slowing down, she would throw her weight forward and pull straight ahead. After they had been out two or three times together, they grew quite friendly.

One day when Ginger and Black Beauty were standing alone in the shade, Ginger asked Black Beauty to tell her all about his bringing up and breaking in. When he had finished she said sadly: "You're lucky! If I'd been treated like that, I might have had as good a temper as you."

Then she told Black Beauty how before she came to Birtwick Park to live she had been forced by a check rein to hold her head up too high for hours at a time, and to wear two sharp bits in her mouth instead of one, and how she had been whipped. Black Beauty felt very sorry for her. As the weeks went by, and she got only good treatment from John and James, he noticed that she began to lose her scary, suspicious look and grow much more gentle and cheerful.

ONE morning in the autumn Black Beauty was harnessed to the dogcart, and the Squire set off on a long journey with John driving. It was late afternoon before the Squire had finished his business and was returning home. Suddenly, as they drove along the edge of a wood, a big storm came up. Trees came crashing down around them, and one fell right across the road in front of the dogcart.

Black Beauty stopped still and trembled, but he did not turn around or run away; he had been brought up not to do that. John jumped down and said, "There, there," and Black Beauty was soothed by the calmness of his voice.

They could not go on, because the fallen tree blocked the road. So they had to turn back and take a longer route home.

It was nearly dark when they reached a small wooden bridge that had to be crossed. The moment Black Beauty's feet touched the planks of the bridge, he felt sure there was something wrong, and he came to a dead stop.

John tried to lead him forward. "Come on, Beauty, what's the matter?"

Of course Black Beauty could not tell him, but he knew very well that the bridge was not safe.

Just then the man at the tollgate at the other end of the bridge ran out, frantically waving a torch about.

"Hoy, hoy, hoy! Halloo! Stop!" he cried.

"What's the matter?" shouted Squire Gordon.

"The bridge is broken in the middle, and part of it has been carried away. If you take another step you'll be in the river!"

"You Beauty!" cried John. "You saved our lives!" He gently turned Black Beauty around and they started off again, taking a different route home.

Black Beauty heard the Squire talking to John. He was glad to learn that by stopping when he did, he had saved them all from being drowned. God, said the Squire, had given men reason, by which they could find out things for themselves, but He had given animals knowledge which did not depend on reason and by which they had often saved the lives of men.

Oh, what a fine supper John gave Black Beauty that night! A nice thick bed of straw, too. And Black Beauty was glad of it, for he was tired.

ONE of the greatest pleasures for the horses was being sad-
dled for a riding party. The master always rode Ginger
and the mistress rode Black Beauty. It was so cheerful to be
trotting and cantering that it always put the two horses in high
spirits. Black Beauty had the best of it, for the mistress's voice
was sweet, and her hand was so light on the reins that he was
guided almost without feeling it.

Oh, Black Beauty used to think, if people only knew what a comfort to horses a light hand is, and how it keeps a horse's mouth in good condition, and the animal himself in a good temper, they surely would not drag and pull at the rein as they often do. Horses' mouths are so tender that where they have not been spoiled or hardened by bad or ignorant treatment, they feel the slightest movement of the driver's hand, and know what the driver wants them to do.

Late one afternoon when Ginger and Black Beauty were brought back to the stables, they noticed that Merrylegs was not yet back in his stall. He had been taken out early in the day by Miss Flora and Miss Jessie and their friends. While Ginger and Black Beauty were still wondering where he could be, James brought him in. As he put the halter on Merrylegs, James said:

"There, you rascal, see that you behave yourself."

"What have you been doing, Merrylegs?" Black Beauty asked.

"Oh!" said he, tossing his little head, "I have only been giving those young people a lesson. They didn't know when they had had enough or when I had had enough, so I just pitched them off backward."

"What!" said Black Beauty. "You threw the children off? Did you throw Miss Jessie or Miss Flora?"

Merrylegs looked very hurt, and said, "Of course not. I am very careful of them. It's the boys. Boys," he said, shaking his mane, "are quite different; they must be broken in as we were

broken in when we were colts, and taught what's what. The other children had ridden me around for nearly two hours, and the boys felt it was their turn. I didn't mind, but when they cut a stick for a riding whip and began beating me with it very hard, I stopped two or three times to let them know I didn't like it. But they didn't seem to understand that  a pony can get tired, or have any feelings; so I just rose up on my hind legs and let the boy who was sitting on me slip off behind—that was all. I had to do it again and again to make them all understand. They're not bad boys; they don't mean to be cruel; but I had to teach them a lesson."

"If I had been you," said Ginger, "I would have given those boys a good kick."

"Oh no," said Merrylegs, "I couldn't do that, after the kind treatment I've had here. Why should I turn nasty because a couple of ignorant boys used me badly? Besides, if I began kicking, the master would sell me, and I might find myself worked to death at some place where no one cared for me. No," shaking his head, "I hope I shall never come to that. But look! Here come the boys with their hands full of apples. I guess it's their way of saying they are sorry for the way they acted."

Ginger and Black Beauty were glad to be with Merrylegs when the boys brought their peace offering, and the three friends enjoyed munching the sweet apples.

A FEW months later James, the stable boy, was allowed to practice driving, for he was soon to take a job as groom at another place. With Ginger and Black Beauty harnessed to the carriage, the master had James take him wherever he wanted to go.

Black Beauty was delighted with the number of places they went to in the city on Saturdays, and the queer streets they were driven through. They were sure to go to the railway station

just as the train was coming in, and cabs and carriages, carts and buses were all trying to get over the bridge together. It was very good practice indeed for James and the two horses.

One day the master and mistress decided to visit friends some distance away. Black Beauty and Ginger were harnessed to the carriage and off they went.

At sundown they stopped for the night at a pleasant hotel which had stables and coachhouses at the farther end of the yard. James saw to it that Black Beauty and Ginger were rubbed down, cleaned and fed. Later in the evening another traveler's horse was brought in, and while the hostler was cleaning him, a young man with a pipe in his mouth lounged into the stable to gossip.

31

"I say, Towler," said the hostler. "Climb up to the loft and throw some hay down for this horse, will you? But put down your pipe first."

"All right," said the young man, and up he went. He tossed down the hay, and soon the horses were alone again. James came in to have a look at Black Beauty and Ginger before going to bed, and then the door was locked.

Black Beauty did not know how long he had slept, or what time it was, but he woke up suddenly feeling very uncomfortable. He heard Ginger coughing, and one of the other horses moved about restlessly. It was dark, and he could see nothing, but the stable was full of smoke and he could hardly breathe.

The trap door to the loft had been left open, and it seemed to Black Beauty that the smoke came from there. He listened and heard a soft rushing sort of noise, and a low crackling and snapping. There was something so strange in the sound that it made him tremble all over. The other horses were all awake now. Some were pulling at their halters, others were stamping.

At last Black Beauty heard steps outside, and the hostler who had put up the last horse burst into the stable with a lantern. He began to untie the horses, to lead them out. But he was in such a hurry and seemed so frightened that he frightened the horses still more.

Not one, not even Black Beauty, would go with him. They were foolish, of course, but danger lay all around, there was nobody with them whom they could trust, and everything was all so strange.

As Black Beauty looked up, he saw a red light flickering on the wall. Then he heard a cry of "Fire! Fire!" outside, and an old hostler came in quickly and quietly. He was so calm that he did not scare the horses. He got one horse out of its stall and went to another.

33

The next thing Black Beauty heard was the voice of James, quiet and cheery as it always was.

"Come, Beauty, on with your bridle, my boy, and we'll soon be out of this smoke."

34

The bridle was on in no time, and then James took the scarf off his neck and tied it lightly over Black Beauty's eyes. Patting and coaxing and speaking gently, he led Black Beauty out of the stable. Safe in the yard, he slipped the scarf off the horse's eyes, and shouted, "Here, somebody! Take this horse while I go back for the other."

A tall man took hold of Black Beauty's bridle, and James darted back into the stable. Black Beauty set up a shrill whinny as he saw him go. Ginger told Black Beauty afterward that his whinnying was the best thing he could have done for her, for if she hadn't heard him outside she would never have had the courage to come out. And Black Beauty told Ginger that he had been frightened, too, but as soon as he had heard James's voice in the stable, he had known they would both be all right, for James was their friend.

By the time the fire engines arrived, James was leading Black Beauty and Ginger to another stable; and there they spent the rest of the night, safe from all danger.

In the morning James went back to the hotel to see about the harness and carriage, and when he returned Black Beauty heard him tell a hostler it was Towler's pipe that had started the fire. Black Beauty remembered John's rule, never to allow a pipe in the stable, and thought it ought to be the rule everywhere.

ONE evening, after the Gordons and Black Beauty and Ginger had returned to Birtwick Park, James and John were talking in the stable.

"Who is going to take my place when I leave?" James asked.

"Little Joe Green at the Lodge," said John.

"Why, he's just a child!" James protested.

"He's fourteen and a half," said John. "He's small, but he's quick and willing and kind-hearted. He wants very much to come, his father would like it, and the master wants to give him his chance, just as he gave me my chance long ago when my father and mother died."

So the next day Joe Green came to the stables to learn all he could before James left. He was a nice bright little fellow, and always came whistling to work.

A few nights after James had left, Black Beauty had eaten his hay and was lying down on his straw fast asleep, when he was suddenly awakened by the loud ringing of the stable bell. He heard the door of John's house open, and then the sound of running feet. In a moment John was in the stable, putting on Black Beauty's saddle and bridle. Up to the door of Birtwick Hall they went together at a quick trot.

The Squire stood there with a lamp in his hand.

"Now, John," he said, "you must ride for your mistress's life. Take this note to Dr. White. Then give your horse a rest at the inn, and be back as soon as you can."

John said, "Yes, sir," and was off in a minute, through the
park and the village, and down the hill to the tollgate. John shouted and thumped on the door, and the man soon came out and
threw open the gate.

"Keep the gate open for the doctor," called John. "Here's the
money," and away he went.

There was a long stretch of level road along the river. John
said, "Now, Beauty, do your best," and Beauty did. He needed
no whip, and for two miles he galloped as fast as if he were in a
race. When they came to the bridge, John pulled him up a little
and patted his neck.

"Well done, old fellow," he said, and then they were off as fast as before. The air was frosty, the moon was bright, and it was very pleasant. They went through another village, through a dark wood, uphill and down, till after an eight miles' run they came to the town. All was still except for the clatter of Black Beauty's feet on the stones. As they drew up at Dr. White's door the clock in the church tower struck three. John rang the bell, and pounded on the door. An upstairs window opened, and out came Dr. White's head.

"What do you want?" he called.

"Mrs. Gordon is very ill, sir. Master wants you to come right away. He thinks she'll die if you can't get there. Here's a note."

"Wait," said the doctor. "I'll be right down." He closed the window, and was soon at the door. "The worst of it is," he said, "my horse has been on the go all day and is worn out. My son has taken the other horse. May I use yours?"

"He has come at a gallop nearly all the way, sir," said John, "and I was to give him a rest here; but I know my master wants you to get there in a hurry, so I guess he would not object."

"All right," said the doctor. "I'll be ready in a minute."

Black Beauty was very hot, and he was glad to stand there while John stroked his neck. Soon the doctor came out with his riding whip.

"You won't need that, sir," said John. "Black Beauty will go till he drops. Take care of him, sir, if you can. I wouldn't want any harm to come to him."

"No, John, of course not," said the doctor.

The way back to Birtwick Hall was even harder. The doctor was a heavier man than John, and not so good a rider; but Black Beauty did his best. Little Joe Green was waiting at the lodge gate, and Squire Gordon was at the Hall door, for he had heard them coming. The doctor went into the house with the Squire, and Joe led Black Beauty to the stable.

Poor Beauty! He was glad to get home, for his legs shook under him, and he could only stand and pant. There was not a dry hair on his body; the water ran down his legs; and he steamed all over. Joe still had much to learn. He rubbed the horse's legs and chest, but he did not cover him with a warm blanket. He thought Black Beauty would be too hot. Then Joe gave him a pail of cold water to drink, put hay and corn in front of him and, thinking he had done the right things, went away.

Soon Black Beauty began to shake and tremble. He felt freezing cold, and he ached all over. Oh, how he wished for his warm thick blanket, and for John to come; but John had eight miles to walk.

Black Beauty lay down on his straw and tried to go to sleep. At last he heard John at the door. He gave a low moan, for he was in great pain. In a moment John was at his side, stooping down over the horse. Black Beauty could not tell him how he felt, but John seemed to know. Quickly he covered the poor horse with two or three blankets, and then ran to the house for hot water. He made some warm gruel which Black Beauty drank. All this time John was talking to himself, and he seemed very angry. "Stupid boy!" he kept saying. "No blanket! And I'll bet the water was cold, too."

Black Beauty was very sick. John nursed him night and day, and the horse doctor came to see him every day. Little Joe Green was broken-hearted to think he had let Black Beauty get sick, all because he did not know the right things to do.

The master came out to the stable often to see his favorite. "My poor Beauty!" he said one day. "My good horse! You saved your mistress's life, Beauty. Yes, you saved her life."

Of course, Black Beauty was very glad to hear that, and slowly he began to get better. Then everyone was happier at Birtwick Hall.

IT was now three years since Black Beauty had come there to live, and he would have liked to stay forever; but sad changes were about to take place. The mistress was not well, and the doctor said she must go away to a warm country for two or three years. Everyone was sorry, for it meant the break-up of Birtwick Hall.

Ginger and Black Beauty were sold to the Squire's friend, the Earl of W——. Merrylegs was given to the Vicar, and Joe Green went along to take care of him. The children came out with their governess to say good-bye to their beloved Merrylegs.

"Have you decided what to do, John?" the master asked.

"Well, sir," said John. "I've made up my mind that if I could get a job with some good horse trainer it would be the right thing for me.

"Many young animals are frightened and spoiled by wrong treatment, and that need not be if the right man took them in hand. I get on well with horses, and if I could help some of them to a fair start I should feel as if I was doing some good."

"Yes," said the master. "You understand horses, and they understand you. I'll do all I can to help you get such a job."

Then came the sad last day at Birtwick Park. Black Beauty and Ginger drove the Gordons to the railroad station and heard the mistress saying, "Good-by, John. God bless you."

The next morning John took Black Beauty and Ginger across country about fifteen miles to Earlshall Park, where the Earl of W—— lived. John patted the horses before he left them, and Black Beauty held his face close to John, for that was all he could do to say good-by.

THE Earl's house was very fine, and there were many stables, but the horses were not as happy as they had been before. They had to wear tight reins that held their heads up too high when they pulled the carriage, and they did not feel that the people around them loved their horses as much as the Gordons did.

When the Earl's family went for a long visit to London, the horses were left in the care of a man named Reuben Smith. Reuben understood horses and was good to them, but he had one great fault—he sometimes got drunk. Because of this he had never been able to get a job as head coachman, but still he was so pleasant and useful that the Earl hoped he could be trusted to take care of the stables while the regular coachman was in London with the Earl's family.

One day Reuben rode Black Beauty to the White Lion Inn, where he told the hostler to feed the horse well. A nail was coming loose in one of Black Beauty's shoes.

"Shall I fix that shoe?" asked the hostler.

"No," said Reuben in a loud voice. "It will be all right till we get home. I'm going to see some of my friends, but I'll be back at six o'clock."

Black Beauty thought it was very unlike Reuben not to see about the shoe, as he was usually very particular about loose nails.

It was nearly nine o'clock when Reuben came back, and he was drunk and in very bad humor.

Almost before they were out of town he began using the whip although Black Beauty was already going at a gallop. The moon had not yet risen, and it was very dark. The roads were stony, and Black Beauty's shoe kept getting looser and looser until it finally came off.

If Reuben had been in his right senses, he would have known something was wrong, but he kept driving ahead at a gallop over sharp stones that cut into Black Beauty's poor foot that had no shoe.

No horse could keep his footing when he was driven like that. Finally Black Beauty stumbled and fell forward on his front knees. Reuben was thrown off, and he lay still on the ground. Black Beauty's knees and foot were hurting very much, but he stood quietly by the edge of the road, waiting for help to come.

46

It was nearly midnight when Robert and Ned, two of the men from Earlshall Park, came up the road in the dogcart with Ginger pulling it. They were coming to see why Reuben had not reached home, and they were much surprised to find his body lying in the road.

"Why, look!" said Ned, seeing Black Beauty's cut knees. "The horse has been down and thrown him! Who would have thought the black horse would do that? Nobody thought he could fall."

Then Robert tried to lead Black Beauty forward, but the horse took one step and almost fell again.

Robert knelt down beside him. "See here! He's hurt in the foot as well as the knees! His hoof is all cut to pieces. No wonder he fell, poor fellow! Reuben must have been out of his senses to think of riding a horse over these stones without a shoe."

They put Reuben into the dogcart, and then Robert tied his handkerchief tightly around Black Beauty's sore foot, and slowly led him home. Feeling sorry for the poor horse, Robert patted him and talked to him all the way. Back in the stable, he bathed and cleaned the wounds and made Black Beauty as comfortable as he could.

The next day the horse doctor came. "I don't think the joints are hurt," he said. "If they aren't, he'll be able to work, but of course he'll never have good-looking knees again."

It took a long time for Black Beauty's wounds to heal, and then he was turned into a meadow for a month or two to rest. One day the Earl came to see him.

"What I feel worst about," the Earl was saying to the coachman, "is that Squire Gordon thought his horses would have a good home with me. And now I'll have to sell this black one. It's a great pity, but I couldn't have knees like those in my stables."

"No, sir," said the coachman, "but I know a man in Bath who has a livery stable. He takes good care of his horses, and he might want to buy this one."

About a week after this, with only a good-by whinny to Ginger, he was put on a train and sent to Bath.

AND now Black Beauty learned that a livery stable was a place where horses and carriages were kept, where anyone who wanted to go riding could come and pay to have a horse for as long as he pleased. Always before, Black Beauty had been driven by people who knew how to drive, but now all kinds of people took him out. Some of them knew very little about horses and held the reins too tight or too loose, and others were always showing off by driving too fast.

It was a hard time for Black Beauty, but he did his best. One day a man who was a good rider took a liking to him and decided to buy him.

So Black Beauty had another master—Mr. Barry, a business man. He hired a stable a short distance from his home, and paid a man named Filcher to look after his horse. Filcher took good care of Black Beauty except for one thing—he didn't give him enough to eat. Black Beauty heard the master order the best of food for him, but where was it all going?

Black Beauty began to grow thin. Mr. Barry rode him out to the country one day to see a friend of his who was a farmer.

The farmer looked closely at Black Beauty.

"What do you feed your horse?" asked the farmer.

"Hay, beans, oats and corn," said Mr. Barry.

"Well, you had better see who is eating your oats and corn," said the farmer, "for I don't think your horse is getting them."

And soon Mr. Barry found out that Filcher was stealing the food and taking it home. He found another groom to take care of Black Beauty, but this man did not keep the stable clean, and Black Beauty's feet became tender and sore from standing on dirty, wet straw. Mr. Barry was so disgusted by his grooms' neglect of their work that he decided to sell his horse.

And so Black Beauty was taken to a Horse Fair to be sold. Here he saw young horses just out of the country, shaggy little Welsh ponies no higher than his old friend Merrylegs, hundreds of cart horses, some like himself who had had some accident, some splendid animals who looked fit for anything, and some poor old horses with all their ribs showing. It made Black Beauty sad to see these last ones.

50

There was a great deal of bargaining going on, and many people came to look at Black Beauty. First they would pull his mouth open, then look at his eyes, then feel his legs and skin, and then try his paces. But what a difference there was in the way these things were done! Some did them in a rough, offhand way; while others would pass their hands gently over his body, with a friendly pat now and then.

There was one man Black Beauty liked right away. He kept hoping this man would buy him. He was rather a small man, but well-made and quick in his motions. His gray eyes were kind and cheerful, and he had a clean, fresh smell about him. Black Beauty could tell by the way he handled him that he was used to horses. The man offered a hundred dollars for Black Beauty, but the salesman said that was not enough. As the little man walked away, Black Beauty looked after him sadly.

51

Then a hard-faced man came along, and he offered a hundred dollars too. Black Beauty did not like this man and hoped he would not get him for a master. In the midst of the bargaining, the little gray-eyed man came back. Black Beauty reached out his head toward him, and the man patted it.

"Well, old chap," he said, "I think we suit each other." Then he spoke to the man in charge: "I'll give a hundred and ten for him."

"Say a hundred and twenty and you can have him."

"A hundred and fifteen," said the little man, and Black Beauty's heart beat for joy when the salesman said, "All right."

The new master was Jerry Barker. After a good feed of oats,

Black Beauty was on his way to London, with Jerry on his back. When they reached the great city, the gas lamps were already lighted. After going through miles of streets, Jerry guided his horse into a narrow alley and pulled up in front of one of the houses. He whistled, and the door of the house flew open. Out ran a pretty young woman, followed by a little girl and a boy. They all threw their arms around Jerry as he got off his horse.

"Now then, Harry, my boy, open the gate, and Mother will bring us the lantern," said Jerry.

The next minute they were all standing around Black Beauty in a small stableyard.

"Is he gentle, Father?" asked the little girl.

"Yes, Dolly, as gentle as your kitten. Come and pat him."

Dolly's little hand reached out to pat Black Beauty's shoulder. How good it felt! Then he was led into a clean and comfortable stable and given plenty of dry straw. After a good supper, he lay down to sleep, feeling that he was going to be happy again.

Jerry Barker, the new master, was a cab driver. His wife, Polly, was a plump little woman with smooth dark hair, dark eyes and a smiling mouth. Harry was nearly twelve, tall and good-natured. Eight-year-old Dolly was just like her mother.

The morning after Black Beauty went to live at the Barkers', Polly and Dolly came out to the yard to make friends. Harry had been there since early morning, helping his father to groom the new horse, and he had already said Black Beauty was "a regular brick." Polly brought an apple, and Dolly had a piece of bread. It was a great treat for Black Beauty to be petted again and talked to in a gentle voice, and he let them see as well as he could that he wanted to be friendly.

That afternoon Jerry made sure the collar and bridle fitted comfortably, and then Black Beauty was hitched to the cab. For the first few days he found his new work very hard. He was not used to London, and the rush and noise of traffic worried him. But he soon found out he could trust Jerry, and that made things easier.

Jerry was a fine man as well as a fine driver. He never used a whip on Black Beauty; he gave him plenty of food and water, cleaned the stable well, and saw to it that Sunday was a day of rest for his horse as well as for himself.

Jerry liked to make up little songs to sing to himself. One he was fond of was this:

> "Come, father and mother,
> "And sister and brother,
> "Come, all of you, turn to
>   And help one another."

54

When he was driving his cab Jerry was just as cheerful and kind, but he would never make Black Beauty go too fast just because someone was impatient. Sometimes, if a passenger was anxious to get somewhere in a hurry, and had a good reason, Jerry would say to Black Beauty, "Come on, my boy! We'll show them how we can get over the ground!" And then they would go like the wind.

On cold, wintry days Dolly would come to the cab stand with some hot soup or pudding for her father; but at Christmas time Jerry and his horse were kept so busy that there was scarcely ever time for them to stop for something to eat.

On New Year's Eve they had to take two men to a party at nine o'clock.

"Come back at eleven," said one of the men. "You may have to wait for a few minutes, but don't be late."

Promptly at eleven o'clock Jerry and Black Beauty were back at the house where they had left the men, but they had to wait and wait out in the cold. For two hours and a half they waited. By the time the passengers finally came out to the cab, Jerry was coughing and Black Beauty's legs were so numb that he almost stumbled; but he managed to pull the carriage until the men were taken home and he and Jerry were back at their own stable.

Jerry was coughing so hard he could hardly speak. Polly came out with the lantern.

"Can't I do something?" she asked anxiously.

"Yes," said Jerry in a hoarse voice. "Give this poor creature something warm, and then please make me some hot soup."

Jerry took time for the usual rubdown, and even went up to the hayloft for an extra bundle of straw for Black Beauty's bed. Polly brought a warm mash for the hungry and tired horse, and then she and Jerry went off to the house.

The next morning it was Harry who came to clean the stable. Black Beauty wondered where Jerry was. At noon Dolly came with Harry to give the horse his food and water. Dolly was crying, and from their talk Black Beauty learned that Jerry was dangerously sick. Many days passed before he began to get better; and then the doctor said he was not strong enough to be a cab driver any longer.

It was arranged that the Barker family should move to the country, where Jerry would have a good job as coachman. This was very sad news for Black Beauty, though, for it meant he would be sold again.

"I wish we could take you with us," whispered Polly when she and the children came to say good-by to the horse. She and Dolly put their faces close to his neck and kissed him. Harry said nothing, but stood there sadly, petting him.

Black Beauty's next master, Nicholas Skinner, was a cab driver, but altogether different from Jerry Barker. There was never any rest for his horses, and Mr. Skinner was always ready to use a whip.

Poor Black Beauty! He was so tired that he wished he could drop down dead, and one day his wish almost came true.

Mr. Skinner had taken him to the railroad station to meet a train. There were four passengers in the party that climbed into Skinner's cab, and they piled so much baggage on top that Black Beauty, already hungry and tired, could hardly pull the cab.

He managed somehow until he came to a steep hill, but there the heavy load was too much for him. Mr. Skinner was using the

whip, and Black Beauty was trying his best, when suddenly his feet slipped from under him and he fell heavily to the ground. As he lay there he could hear voices saying, "The poor horse! He's dead! He'll never get up again."

Then somebody threw cold water on his head, poured medicine into his mouth, and covered him with a blanket. After a while he felt a little stronger. He staggered to his feet and was led to a stable, where a warm drink was brought to him. He drank it gratefully.

By evening Black Beauty was able to go back to Skinner's stable, and the horse doctor came to see him.

"If he could have six months' rest he'd be of some use again," said the horse doctor, "but he has been worked too hard, and there isn't any strength left in him."

"I can't afford to let him rest that long," said Mr. Skinner in his rough way.

"Well," said the doctor, "there's going to be a sale of horses in about ten days. Feed him well and let him rest till the sale, and you might get something for him."

So once again Black Beauty went to a horse sale, holding up his head and hoping for the best. Some of the people who came to examine him looked not much better off than the poor horses they were bargaining about. Then Black Beauty noticed a nice-looking old farmer with a little boy. The farmer was wearing a broad-brimmed hat, and beneath it his round, ruddy face shone out kindly.

"There's a horse, Willie, that has known better days," said the farmer, reaching out his hand to pat Black Beauty. And Black Beauty pushed his nose forward as if in answer to this kindness.

"Poor old fellow!" said Willie, stroking Black Beauty's face.

"See, Grandfather, how well he understands kindness. Oh, Grandfather, please buy him and make him well again."

The farmer could not make up his mind right away, but Willie kept on talking about Black Beauty's good points until finally the old man paid twenty-five dollars for the horse and took him home.

Mr. Thoroughgood was the farmer's name. He and his grandson Willie came every day to see how Black Beauty was getting along in the pleasant meadow where he was turned loose. The perfect rest, the good food, the soft grass and gentle exercise soon began to tell on Black Beauty's condition and spirits; and by the next spring his legs had improved so much that he seemed quite young again.

Mr. Thoroughgood and Willie tried him out one day in the carriage, and were much pleased with him. Black Beauty did so well that the farmer decided to find a good home for him.

Early in the summer there came a day when Black Beauty was cleaned with special care and taken to a pretty little house a mile or two from the village.

"I hope the ladies will like him," said Mr. Thoroughgood.

"Oh, I hope so, too," said Willie, "because this would be such a good home for him, and I could come to see him often."

Then three ladies came out to look at the horse. They decided to keep him on trial.

"If you don't like him, send him back to me," said Mr. Thoroughgood.

Black Beauty was taken to a comfortable stable, fed, and left to himself.

The next day, when the groom was cleaning his face, he said, "This is just like the star that Black Beauty had. I wonder where he is now." A little farther on, he came to a small scar on the horse's neck. The groom looked surprised. He went over Black Beauty carefully, talking to himself.

"White star on his forehead, one white foot, this little scar—" then, looking at the middle of the horse's back "—and here's that little patch of white hair. It *must* be Black Beauty! Oh, Beauty, Beauty, do you remember me—little Joe Green, who almost killed you?" And he began patting the horse all over.

Black Beauty couldn't really remember him, for Joe had grown up and now had black whiskers and a deep voice; but Black Beauty put his nose up to him as if to say they were friends.

"I wonder who broke your knees, old Beauty," said Joe. "You must have had a bad time of it somewhere, but you're going to have *good* times now. I wish John were here to see you."

The ladies were just as pleased as Joe was when he told them he was sure their horse was Squire Gordon's Black Beauty.

"I'll write to Mrs. Gordon," said one of the sisters. "How glad she will be to know that her favorite horse has come to us!"

And so Black Beauty found a happy home. The ladies liked him so well that they promised never to sell him. Since his work was pleasant and easy, his strength and spirits all came back again. Joe Green was the best and kindest of grooms, and Willie came to see him often. His troubles were over, and he was at home. Often, before he was quite awake, he imagined he was still in the orchard at Birtwick, standing with his old friends under the apple trees.

RANDOM HOUSE BOOKS FOR CHILDREN

Question and Answer Books

For ages 6-10:
Question and Answer Book of Nature
Question and Answer Book of Science
Question and Answer Book of Space
Question and Answer Book About the
　Human Body

Gateway Books

For ages 8 and up:
The Friendly Dolphins
The Horse that Swam Away
Champ: Gallant Collie
Mystery of the Musical Umbrella
and other titles

Step-Up Books

For ages 7-8:
Animals Do the Strangest Things
Birds Do the Strangest Things
Fish Do the Strangest Things
Meet Abraham Lincoln
Meet John F. Kennedy
and other titles

Babar Books

For ages 4 and up:
The Story of Babar
Babar the King
The Travels of Babar
Babar Comes to America
and other titles

Books by Dr. Seuss

For ages 5 and up:
Dr. Seuss's Sleep Book
Happy Birthday to You!
Horton Hatches the Egg
Horton Hears a Who
If I Ran the Zoo
I Had Trouble in Getting to Solla
　Sollew
McElligot's Pool
On Beyond Zebra
Scrambled Eggs Super!
The Sneetches
Thidwick: The Big-Hearted Moose
Yertle the Turtle
and other titles

Giant Picture Books

For ages 5 and up:
Abraham Lincoln
Big Black Horse
Big Book of Things to Do and
　Make
Big Book of Tricks and Magic
Blue Fairy Book
Daniel Boone
Famous Indian Tribes
George Washington
Hiawatha
King Arthur
Peter Pan
Robert E. Lee
Robin Hood
Robinson Crusoe
Three Little Horses
Three Little Horses at the King's
　Palace

Beginner Books

For ages 5-7:
The Cat in the Hat Beginner Book
　Dictionary
The Cat in the Hat
The Cat in the Hat Comes Back
Dr. Seuss's ABC Book
Green Eggs and Ham
Go, Dog, Go!
Bennett Cerf's Book of Riddles
The King, the Mice and the Cheese
and other titles

Picture Books

For ages 4 and up:
Poems to Read to the Very Young
Songs to Sing with the Very Young
Stories to Read to the Very Young
Alice in Wonderland
Anderson's Fairy Tales
Bambi's Children
Black Beauty
Favorite Tales for the Very Young
Grandmas and Grandpas
Grimm's Fairy Tales
Heidi
Little Lost Kitten
Mother Goose
Once-Upon-A-Time Storybook
Pinocchio
Puppy Dog Tales
Read-Aloud Nursery Tales
Sleeping Beauty
The Sleepytime Storybook
Stories that Never Grow Old
The Wild and Wooly Animal Book
The Wizard of Oz

Black Beauty